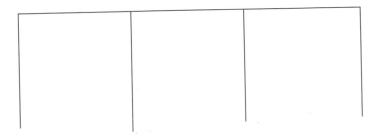

WHERE IS FRED?

To Eileen
– my lovely bit of fluff E.H.

To Matt, Kirsten,
Ansel and Toby A.P.

EGMONT
We bring stories to life

First published in Great Britain 2012
by Egmont UK Limited
239 Kensington High Street
London W8 6SA

Text copyright © Edward Hardy 2012
Illustrations copyright © Ali Pye 2012

The moral rights of the author and illustrator have been asserted

ISBN 978 1 4052 5402 1 (Hardback)
ISBN 978 1 4052 5403 8 (Paperback)

1 2 3 4 5 6 7 8 9 10

www.egmont.co.uk

A CIP catalogue record for this title is available
from the British Library

Printed and bound in Singapore

47225/1/2

Visit Edward at www.kissyhuggra.com   and Ali at www.alipye.com

WHERE IS FRED?

by Edward Hardy

Illustrated by

Ali Pye

EGMONT

There once was a
lovely fluffy white
caterpillar called Fred.

Look at how
lovely and fluffy he is.
You can stroke him
if you like.

Fred was a very
happy little caterpillar.
He loved playing games.

His favourite game
was Hide-and-Seek.

It was a game
he was **very
good at**.

Here he is
hiding in a pile
of cotton-wool balls.

Here he is
floating on a cup
of frothy milk.

And here he is sitting
on a fluffy white sheep.

Indeed, when you are a
small juicy caterpillar,
it is a VERY GOOD IDEA
to stay hidden.

But Fred could not spend
all his time hiding. In fact,
he, like all caterpillars,
spent most of his day
eating leaves.

Lovely shiny green leaves.

Here is Fred on a bush.

You can see the problem.

But was Fred frightened?
Not in the least.

Then one day,
Fred looked up from
a leaf and saw something
he had never seen before.

And what he saw
made him
VERY
FRIGHTENED
INDEED.

GERALD

THE

CROW!

"KAWRAARRRHHH!"

"YIKES!" said Fred.

And off he scarpered,
as fast as his little legs
could carry him.

Gerald flew off after Fred.

On the High Street, he came across
a smart-looking woman,
in a navy suit and a
lovely fluffy white
necklace.

"Have you seen a fluffy white
caterpillar?" squawked Gerald.
"I want him for my lunch!"

"Sorry," replied the woman. "I'm afraid I haven't."

"Are you sure?" asked Gerald, examining her necklace,
which seemed *somewhat* familiar.

"Quite sure," said the woman.

"BOTHER!"

said Gerald.

And off he flew.

In the park, Gerald spotted
a man with grey straggly hair
and lovely fluffy white
eyebrows
. . . that joined in the middle.

"Have you seen a fluffy white
caterpillar?" croaked Gerald.
"I want him for my lunch!"

"No," replied the man.
"I'm afraid I haven't."

"Are you *sure*?" asked Gerald,
examining the man's eyebrows,
which seemed *strangely* familiar.

"Quite sure," said the man.

"DRAT!" said Gerald.
And off he flew.

At the nursery, Gerald spotted
a little girl in a pretty **pink** dress,
and a **lovely fluffy white**
hairband.

"Have you seen a fluffy white
caterpillar?" cawed Gerald.
"I want him for my lunch!"

"Oh no," replied the little girl.
"There are *no* caterpillars here."

"Are you sure?"
asked Gerald,
poking a pointy claw
at the girl's hairband,
which seemed
remarkably familiar.

"Quite sure," said the girl.

**"DOUBLE
DRAT!"**
said Gerald.

And off he flew.

At the fairground, Gerald met a man sporting a red velvet waistcoat and a lovely fluffy white moustache.

"Have you seen a fluffy white caterpillar?" shrieked Gerald. "I want him for my lunch!"

"Terribly sorry," replied the man. "I'm afraid I haven't."

Now, Fred, who up until this moment had managed to stay **absolutely** still, started to think how terribly clever he had been to hide from this ridiculous bird.

And as he looked at Gerald, hopping furiously from one foot to the other, he began to giggle.

And as he
giggled,
he wriggled.

And as he wriggled,
his **lovely fluffy white** hairs
tickled the man
under his nose.

And the man,
"ah . . . ah . . ."

after some **considerable** struggle,

"AAAHHH . . .
AHAHAHAHAAA . . ."

sneezed!

"AAAA TISSSSSHHHH OOOOOO!"

Fred, so small and so light, was tossed

UP . . .

up . . .

UP INTO THE AIR.

"I've got you!" screeched Gerald triumphantly, swooping towards the helpless caterpillar.

At that very moment,
a gust of wind caught Fred,
and lifted him higher and higher into the sky.

Flapping his wings furiously,
Gerald chased him.

But the caterpillar was nowhere to be seen amongst all those lovely fluffy white clouds.

Gerald searched and searched, but he could not find Fred.

"WHERE IS FRED?"

When finally the wind dropped,

the crow flapped back down to the ground,

dizzy and despondent.

"*Where* is Fred?"
he muttered miserably,
looking all around.
But there was no sign of Fred.
No sign at all.

Gerald bowed his head in despair.

And as he looked down,
he noticed that he was
now wearing
the most . . .

lovely

fluffy

white

scarf.

It was beautiful and soft, and he
found it cosy and comforting to wear.

"I wonder where it came from?"
he thought.

Gerald was not the cleverest of birds.

Gerald was so fond of his new scarf
that he was keen to show it off
to the other crows.

They all admired it.
Even though one or two of them
found it *curiously* familiar.

Until one day,
Gerald looked down to discover
that the scarf had vanished.

And in its place, to his delight, he found a
lovely fluffy white . . .

BOW
TIE.